Kestrels 1

The Special Pony

Other Patricia Leitch stories you will enjoy

The Kestrels series

1: The Special Pony
2: A Pony to Jump

The Jinny series

1: For Love of a Horse
2: A Devil to Ride
3: The Summer Riders
4: Night of the Red Horse
5: Gallop to the Hills
6: Horse in a Million
7: The Magic Pony
8: Ride Like the Wind
9: Chestnut Gold
10: Jump for the Moon
11: Horse of Fire
12: Running Wild

Kestrels 1

The Special Pony

Patricia Leitch

Illustrated by Elsie Lennox

Lions
An Imprint of HarperCollins*Publishers*

This series is for Meg

The Special Pony was first published in Lions in 1992
Lions is an imprint of HarperCollins Children's Books
a division of HarperCollins Publishers Ltd,
77–85 Fulham Palace Road, Hammersmith,
London W6 8JB

Printed and bound in Great Britain by
HarperCollins Book Manufacturing Ltd, Glasgow

Chapter One

The Lorimer family all shared the same dream. They all dreamt that some day, when they had a lot of money, they would buy Kestrels and live there. Kestrels was a stone mansion house with battlements and a high stone tower. It was surrounded with overgrown gardens and at one side there was a field that was just meant for horses. It was built on a peninsula of land jutting out into the sea – almost an island – only joined to the mainland by a long, broad avenue, lined by copper beach trees.

Mr Lorimer, who was a librarian, imagined himself turning the wilderness grounds into a garden growing fruit and vegetables and flowers. Mrs Lorimer saw herself filling store cupboards with jars of homemade jam, pickles, bottled fruit and wine; and her deep freeze with vegetables; or sitting at the top of the tower painting the views of sea and countryside.

Ben Lorimer who was fifteen – tall for his age with a shock of black hair like his father's – wanted a room to himself, a room lined with shelves for his books, a room where no one would disturb him.

Emma Lorimer was twelve. She had long fair hair and a happy, easy-going nature. She saw Kestrels as a place where all her friends could come and stay, where there would be music and fun.

Jamie Lorimer was four and the youngest Lorimer. He imagined life at Kestrels being nothing but swimming with one foot securely on the sand, ice cream and sand castles.

Meg Lorimer was a black and white Bearded Collie. She was twelve years old and spent most of her waking hours staring at things and barking for attention. Misty Lorimer was a light grey and white Beardie. She was five, with big brown eyes gleaming through her shaggy face, and she loved to run: if you looked away for a second Misty was off on some private exploration of her own.

But Sally Lorimer, who was nine – medium height, not small not tall; medium size, not fat not skinny; with thick brown hair straight to her shoulders and cut into a fringe, wide-set blue eyes and a quirky mouth that turned up at the corners – Sally longed to live at Kestrels more than all her family put together. Because no one, but absolutely no one, could live in a house that had looseboxes, outbuildings and a field that only needed fencing to turn it into a perfect pony field; no one could live at Kestrels and not have a pony.

In case her father should forget that Sally wanted a pony more than anything else in the world Sally mentioned it to him quite often but she hadn't really much hope. The Lorimers lived in Matwood, a suburb of Tarent in the north west of Scotland and the squashed back garden of their semi-detached house was not really the place for a pony, nor were the busy local roads much good for riding. Even Miss Meek's riding school, where Sally rode when she had saved up enough pocket money, was only two bare fields wired off into grazing strips and a rutted lane that the school horses knew so well they could almost take the rides themselves – up and down, up and down the lane.

When Sally had first seen Kestrels she had known at once that this was the place for her horses – the imaginary horses that she rode everywhere. She saw Starfire, her chestnut stallion, standing in the field with proudly arched neck and alert ears, while Biddy, her trusty bay mare, dozed in the shadow of the chestnut tree as Sally trotted Lucia, her snow white mare, up the long avenue under the purple shadows of the beeches, Meg and Misty leaping beside.

But that was only make-believe.

The Lorimers had discovered Kestrels a year before. They had been looking for a new picnic place when Mr Lorimer stopped the car at the gates of Kestrels. A cracked, weatherbeaten notice board said that the house was for sale although the estate agent's name had almost vanished and the board telling them that trespassers would be prosecuted was lying half-hidden in the long grass.

"Shall we have a look?" Mrs Lorimer asked, peering up the long avenue.

"Why not?" Mr Lorimer said and they all piled out of the car.

They walked for the first time under the beeches and up to the securely locked oak door at the foot of the tower. Four windows stretched above them to the top of the tower and to the right and left ivy-covered walls reached up to the battlements. At either side of the door were two huge stone dogs. One sitting upright, the other lying down with its massive head stretched out on massive paws.

"Like the dogs in the Hans Anderson fairy tale," said Ben as Meg and Misty sniffed them suspiciously.

They walked round the house to the right of the tower and found themselves in a cobbled stableyard. Down one side were four looseboxes and on the other side a range of stable buildings.

"*The* place for your pony," Em said to Sally.

But Sally was standing wide-eyed and unbelieving. To live at Kestrels and have your own stableyard! For a moment she had thought she saw shadowy heads, gazing with gentle eyes over half doors; had thought she heard hooves trampling on straw, then the air quivered and they were gone. Sally rubbed her eyes, not knowing whether she had seen horses that had been stabled there in the past or glimpsed the future horses who would come one day to stand in these empty boxes.

There was a walled garden, festooned with roses and drenched in their scent; a ruined conservatory of broken glass and twisted metal and a vegetable garden still growing rhubarb and potatoes amongst the weeds. At the back of the house a field that had once been spreading lawns reached down to a desolate summerhouse that perched high above the sea.

For a long moment the Lorimers stood in the summerhouse surrounded by sea and sky in a glory of light and space, staring out into the silence.

Then Mrs Lorimer turned to her husband and said, "We must buy it. We must come and live here. Oh Rob, we must," almost as if she had been Sally pleading desperately for a pony.

But when Mr Lorimer tracked down the

estate agent who was selling Kestrels it was so terribly expensive that they all knew they could never afford to buy it.

"When we win the pools," Mrs Lorimer said, defeated.

" 'Spect there would have been mice," Em said, consoling herself.

"And ghosts," Ben added. "Clanking of chains in the tower."

Only Sally had not given in. Whenever the thought of Kestrels came into her head she was riding her own pony up the avenue to where her whole family leant over the battlements waving down to her. She saw it all in colour. Her pony was dapple grey with a white mane and tail.

She was sure it must happen. Sure they would live at Kestrels . . . one day.

Chapter Two

The Lorimers had their first picnic of the year at Fintry Bay, a sandy beach close to Kestrels. It was a day of blue sky and the sun felt warm for the first time in months.

Mr Lorimer pulled his tweed cap over his eyes and lay back on the sand while Mrs Lorimer got out her watercolours and covered pages of her sketch pad with blues and yellows. Ben sat on the sea wall reading, pretending he didn't belong to his family. Em went in for a four-second swim, came out blue and frozen, telling them all how super it was and how they should all go in. Jamie made sandcastles, sat on a jellyfish, screamed and then made more sandcastles. The Beardies barked and leapt and barked. They plunged through the seaweed, found a very dead seagull and rolled in it and had to be taken into the sea by Em.

All afternoon Sally sat with her arms wrapped round her knees watching the path that came down onto the beach. It was the way the riding school came when they rode on the sands. Sally had seen them quite often. The girl who took the rides was very slim with tanned skin and dark hair. She wore a black jacket and boots with cream jodhs. Usually she rode a well-schooled, black horse with one white sock and a broad white blaze but once Sally had seen her on a chestnut that bucked and reared when he felt the sand under his hooves. The girl had controlled him effortlessly, telling the ride to trot on, while she steadied the chestnut to a long, striding walk.

The riders were always smartly turned out and their horses shone with grooming and good feeding. Not in the least like Miss Meek's dusty ponies.

But today there was no sign of the riding school, only a girl on a bay cob had cantered past.

"Time we were making a move?" Mr Lorimer asked, not moving himself.

"Well if we're going round to Kestrels . . ." said Mrs Lorimer.

But still nobody moved. The low sun was warm. The road back home would be busy.

"Four months since we've seen Kestrels," Sally thought. "Anything could have happened. It could have been sold or it might have been pulled down and little bungalows built in its place."

Sally pictured it standing gaunt and empty, unloved. She whispered the name Starfire, and her chestnut stallion came skimming over the sands. Sally leapt onto his back and in seconds she was cantering up the avenue to Kestrels.

"Hand me those boxes," her mother said, shattering Sally's dream.

Sally handed the sandwich boxes over to her mother and stood up.

"Where are you going to?" her mother asked, as if Sally might have been setting off for Mars.

"Just down to the sea."

"Don't be long then. We're going."

Sally scuffed her bare feet through the sands and paddled through the crimpling froth of the waves. Not to be living at Kestrels seemed such a stupid waste. She didn't want to go back to their brick box home. She wanted to live by the sea for always. To catch her dapple grey pony, not a pretend pony but a real pony, and ride bareback over the sands, her pony's silver mane and tail flowing out behind it as they galloped.

Suddenly the setting sun tipped the horizon and instantly a path of golden light stretched out from the sun to the foam's edge.

"Sally come on," called her mother. "Hurry up."

Sally hardly heard her. She turned to face the sun and standing in the sea, facing the golden light, she opened her arms wide.

"A pony," she said aloud. "I Sally Lorimer wish for a pony."

"Goofball," said Ben's voice behind her. "What would you do if a pony came trotting out of the waves? Keep it in the garage?"

Sally hunched her shoulders against her brother's stupidity. For of course she would keep it at Kestrels.

Reluctantly she turned to go. She took one last blinding look at the sun, then, as she turned away, something glittering under the water caught her eye. She crouched down to pick it up and the movement of the sea carried it into the palm of her open hand, almost as if it had swum there by itself. Sally lifted her hand out of the water and lying in the very centre of her palm was a crystal unicorn.

It was about two centimetres high with a gold horn and a gold tassle on its tail. The tiny jewels that were its eyes glinted red and green. It was not chipped or broken in any way.

"What have you found?" Ben demanded.

"Nothing," said Sally, closing her hand and spinning round. She raced across the sands to where her family were organizing the car.

"Some pong from those Beardies," said Mr Lorimer when at last they were all packed in and the two dogs were mounded together between the back seat and the hatchback, in a wet seaweedy mass of grey and black hair.

Sally stretched her arm over the back seat, trying to reach Meg and give her a comforting scratch.

"Don't stir them up," said her mother. "Let them settle."

"Are we going home past Kestrels?" asked her father, knowing the answer before he asked.

"But of course," said Em.

"Yes. Yes. Yes," said Sally.

"I think we might," said Mrs Lorimer.

Ben nodded his head, not looking up from his book. Only Jamie said nothing. He was asleep.

As they drove along the shore road to Kestrels they gradually stopped talking, each thinking the same thing, but afraid to say it aloud. It was months since they had seen Kestrels and every hour of every day had been an hour when someone else might have bought their house.

But when Mr Lorimer stopped at the rusted gates the For Sale board was still there.

"What will we do," said Em, speaking for them all, "when we come and the board has gone?"

"Go home and get our supper," said Ben. "I'm starving."

"Oh no!" cried Sally. "Can't we just walk round once? Please?"

"No," said her mother. "It really is too late. Now that spring's here we'll be able to come any time but better not tonight. Anyway we know that it's not sold and that's the main thing."

Sally stared down the long, mossy avenue, fighting back tears, not wanting to let anyone see that she was nearly crying. "Oh please?" she pleaded, but her father was already looking over his shoulder to make sure the road was clear.

Suddenly Sally remembered the unicorn. She put her hand in her anorak pocket and felt it tiny and magical and instantly, instead of feeling sad at leaving Kestrels without even walking up to the house, she was filled with fizzy, undeserved happiness.

"Look Sally, a pony," said her mother.

Coming up the road was a girl of about Sally's age riding a finely bred roan pony. The girl was lean and tall. She sat easily astride her pony, riding with a relaxed confidence. Her black hard hat had aged to shades of green and was held on top of her sunburst of corn coloured hair by black elastic under her chin. Although her jeans and checked shirt were shabby, her tack was polished and her pony was fit and well groomed. Dazzles of white flickered over his sleek brownish-grey quarters. His hooves were oiled. His pulled mane and wisped tail fell in silken, separate hairs. Thinking of the riding school ponies

Sally was filled with admiration. The roan pony was more like a miniature racehorse than a child's pony.

Seeing that Mr Lorimer was about to drive away the girl halted her pony and, smiling at them with an ear to ear grin, she waved Mr Lorimer on. Sally, pushing Meg and Misty aside, rubbed the steamed-up rear window clear and watched the girl as they drove away.

"She's going to Kestrels!" she exclaimed.

"So she is," said Em. "Cheek of her riding down to our house."

"Probably just going for a ride round," said Mrs Lorimer. "I expect there are masses of people think of Kestrels as their own."

But Sally wasn't listening, she was trotting Starfire beside the roan pony, riding as effortlessly and as confidently as the girl with her explosion of dark golden hair.

That night before she went to sleep Sally placed the little unicorn on her windowsill. Rays of the street lamp caught it, making it shimmer with rainbows.

"So special a thing," Sally thought, gazing at it. "So magical a thing to come especially to me. Anything, anything, could happen now."

Chapter Three

The next magic thing happened on Friday morning. Mr Lorimer and Ben had already left – Mr Lorimer to his library and Ben to his grammar school. Mrs Lorimer, who helped at Jamie's nursery school, was frantically trying to find red things for the red corner. Jamie was eating fistfuls of cornflakes from the packet. Em was checking through her school bag to make sure that she had everything, while Sally was searching madly for her spelling book.

"I must find it. It must be somewhere. Miss MacGregor will climb the curtains if I don't have it," moaned Sally.

"Have you tried under your bed?" suggested

her mother just as there was a loud ring at the door.

"See who's there," Mrs Lorimer said.

When Sally opened the door it was the postman. He had two brown envelopes in his hand and one large white one.

"Is your dad there?" he asked, giving Sally the two brown envelopes. "He's got to sign for this one. Something special."

Mrs Lorimer came to sign for the letter. Sally took it from the postman. It wasn't only the size that was special, everything about it was totally different from her father's usual letters. It was made of very white, very thick paper. Mr Lorimer's name and address had been typed by the kind of typewriter that made it look as if it was printed and on the back flap the name of the sender was pressed into the soft paper.

Mark & Roth Goodchild,
Solicitors,
9 Bream Place,
Tarent G69 4X2.

"Glory look at the time," screamed Mrs Lorimer, snatching the envelope from Sally and standing it on the mantelpiece. "And I've got the keys! Hordes of little horrors stranded on the pavement. Now come on!"

"But I haven't got my spelling book . . ."

"Then you'll need to share."

"But Miss MacGregor . . ."

"Out," said their mother, snatching Jamie up under her arm.

"OUT!" she commanded, pushing the girls through the door and locking it behind her.

"What's in the letter?" Em asked as they bustled along the pavement.

"Probably the Income Tax. Fed up with him not paying. Send him to prison for years. We'll all end up tenting out in the park."

Sally, astride her chestnut stallion, wondered how her mother could be so dim. For of course the envelope was nothing like the Income Tax letters. They were mean and nasty and always caused trouble. This envelope could have come from the Queen.

Mrs Lorimer and Jamie turned left to their nursery school. Em and Sally went straight on towards their concrete-and-glass school building. Now her mother had left them Sally let Starfire gallop on the spot. His silver shoes struck sparks from the pavement and his wild whinnyings soared above the brick houses, above the church steeple, and up to the golden disc of the Sun God. Mrs Lorimer wouldn't let Sally imagine she was riding wild, uncontrollable horses. She wasn't even too keen on Sally trotting along on a quiet pony. But Em didn't mind.

"Watch out for the traffic," Em said when Starfire shied into the street.

"He can't bear it when he sees school."

"Then let him go," suggested Em and Sally slid down from Starfire's back and stood still to watch her fiery stallion rear and plunge before he went soaring over the roof tops to Kestrels and the sea.

"Here," said Em, giving Sally her spelling book. "Take mine. Tell Miss MacGregor that we got them mixed up. She won't mind that so much."

"But what about you?"

"Mr Campbell won't bother. I know my words so he'll never notice."

Spelling was the first lesson after school dinner.

"Hold up your spelling books," said Miss MacGregor.

All the spelling books were green except

Sally's which was blue. Miss MacGregor's gimlet eyes spotted it at once.

"Em and I got them mixed up," explained Sally, waiting for thunderbolts to crash about her, ready to call down Starfire to defend her.

Miss MacGregor took the book from Sally.

"I can remember that happening when my sister and I were at school together," she said and opening the spelling book she began to ask them words from Em's book. Only the brains in the top group could spell them but it didn't matter because they hadn't been homework words, so no one got into trouble and Miss MacGregor was happy thinking about the past.

They got out at four. Em's class had been at the playing fields so Sally walked home alone thinking about the letter. Meg and Misty, flopped at the back door, rose up to meet her with licks and paws. Sally sat down on the step and hugged them.

"Your school skirt," yelled her mother.

"Sorry. Forgot."

Meg and Misty followed Sally into the kitchen.

The envelope was still on the mantelpiece.

"Dad wasn't home at lunchtime?" Sally asked.

"This is his early night," said her mother.

Mr Lorimer and Ben arrived home at twenty to five.

"There's a letter for you," said Sally and Em as Mrs Lorimer came running downstairs to tell her husband the same thing.

"Steady on," said Mr Lorimer, disentangling himself from Jamie's rugby tackle embrace.

He took the letter and turned it over in his hands, reading the solicitor's name and address.

"Oh open it, open it," said Mrs Lorimer. "We've been waiting all day to find out what's in it."

"To do honour to this envelope I need a paperknife."

Sally brought a knife from the kitchen drawer.

"And my glasses."

"Where?" said Mrs Lorimer.

"Brief case."

Mrs Lorimer found them and gave them to him.

Mr Lorimer put them on and with a grand gesture slit the envelope open with the kitchen knife. Very slowly he unfolded the sheet of thick white paper and read the letter aloud.

" 'Dear Sir, If you would contact me at the above address you will learn something to your advantage. As it is a matter of some urgency I would be obliged if you would contact me as soon as possible. Graham Goodchild.' "

"Could it be the Income Tax?" demanded Em anxiously.

" 'To your advantage,' " said Ben. "It means it's good news."

"I don't believe it," said Mr Lorimer. "Letters like this only happen in books."

The Beardies sensed the excitement and rioted round, barking at full blast.

"Get to the phone quick. It's only five to five. You might just catch them before they close," and Mrs Lorimer pushed her husband out into the hall to the phone.

Mr Lorimer dialled the solicitor's number.

"Shut those dogs up. I can't hear . . . Oh yes, yes. Hullo. Hullo. It's Mr Lorimer speaking," said Mr Lorimer, signalling wildly to his wife and Em to remove the Beardies.

Em grabbed Meg and Mrs Lorimer dragged Misty back into the kitchen.

Sally was still sitting on the edge of the table. To her the letter sounded like the beginning of a unicorn magic. A magic that might mean more riding lessons at Miss Meek's or even a new jacket. She didn't dare to think that it might be a strong enough magic to mean a pony.

"They've been trying to trace me for weeks," said Mr Lorimer, coming back into the kitchen. "It was Mr Goodchild himself who spoke to me. Wouldn't tell me anything at all over the phone but he's opening up the office tomorrow morning so he can see me at eleven o'clock."

"What can it be?" said Mrs Lorimer.

"I have no idea," said Mr Lorimer.

All night long Sally tossed and turned, trying to imagine what vitally important thing the solicitor was going to tell her father. She got up at six and took the dogs for a walk in the rough ground behind the school playground. Misty did her usual disappearing act, vanishing into thin air while Sally was tying her shoelace. For half an hour Sally searched and called, part of her furious that Misty had managed to get away and part of her desperately worried in case she should wander onto the road and be run over.

At last Misty reappeared wriggling her way through somebody's hedge. Her shaggy coat was wattled with mud and marigolds. She carried the crust of a loaf clamped firmly between her jaws.

"Where have you been?" raged Sally. "You wicked, wicked dog. Come here at once."

Misty advanced, one paw at a time, gulping down the bread.

Sally pounced and clipped on her lead.

"Does Meg ever go off on her own like that?" Sally demanded as she marched both dogs home. "No, It's always you. Dogging off. You are BAD."

Misty smiled up at her, eyes wide, tail wagging uncertainly.

"Bad," repeated Sally but a smile was creeping into her voice. Really Misty was her favourite.

Mr Lorimer left for Tarent at half-past nine. When Sally had tidied her bedroom she went over to the riding school to fill in the time until her father got back.

A ride was just ready to leave the yard. Miss Meek was sitting solid and secure on a bay hunter called Fred.

"How would you like to square up the boxes," she called down to Sally.

Sally nodded but stood watching the ride leave the yard. The boy on Tansy had one stirrup shorter than the other. Jane Ford who was riding Clover, Sally's favourite pony, had her heels clamped against Clover's sides and her reins gathered up in a stranglehold that pulled the bit back against Clover's mouth. Prince and Princess were already lagging behind, ignoring their riders' crops and heels. They knew that if they stayed far enough behind the rest they wouldn't have to go to the end of the lane.

As Sally turned away to find a brush she saw clearly the girl's roan pony, full of life and energy, trotting under the beeches to Kestrels.

Sally had just finished the three looseboxes when the ride came back. She helped the boy on Tansy to dismount; held Mint's leading rein until Miss Meek took it from her. Her watch said twelve o'clock. There was a chance that her father might be home.

At first Sally galloped home on Starfire but somehow today she couldn't be bothered. Abandoning her stallion she ran full tilt for home, her hand in her anorak pocket clenched round the nugget of the unicorn. Her sandalled feet splatting down on the pavement as she raced along.

Sally had almost reached their house when her father drew up at the gate. Instead of getting out her father just sat behind the wheel. The expression on his face was a blank mask of bewilderment. Even when he saw Sally he didn't smile or wave. He just sat staring through the windscreen. "Dad! Hi Dad," Sally shouted. She had never seen her father like this before and didn't know what to do. She couldn't go on into the house and leave him sitting in the car.

"Dad?" she said again, uncertainly, but still Mr Lorimer paid no attention to her. It was only when the Beardies came bounding and barking down the path that Mr Lorimer got out of the car.

"Be quiet," he yelled at the dogs. "Shut the noise."

"What did he say? What's to your advantage?" Sally demanded.

Mr Lorimer shut the gate, keeping Meg and Misty in. He caught Sally round the waste and threw her into the air as if she were Jamie.

"Come on in," he said catching her again. "Then I'll tell you."

And as they ran up the path together he was laughing and laughing as if he would never stop.

Chapter Four

Mrs Lorimer was standing at the sink peeling potatoes. Jamie was sitting on the floor with one potato and a blunt knife, helping her.

"Well?" she demanded.

"Are you sitting comfortably?" asked her husband.

"Don't be daft! Tell me!"

Ben, hearing his father's voice, came racing down from his room, Em following him.

Mr Lorimer drew in a deep breath.

"I've been left a considerable sum of money," he said.

"You've what?" said his wife.

"The solicitor's own words. 'A considerable sum of money.' In fact you might say quite a lot of money."

"Get on with you," said Mrs Lorimer. "You're joking."

"How much?" said Ben.

"A considerable sum," repeated Mr Lorimer, and Sally saw a quick glance pass between her parents and knew that the details of the considerable amount was not going to be family information.

Mrs Lorimer sat down hard on a chair.

"I do not believe it. It couldn't happen to us."

"It's happened. Dad's Great Uncle Nathan died last December. I hardly knew him. He went off to Australia when he was sixteen. Came back to see us twice. He had red hair and took me to a football match and that's all I remember about him. Used to send us a Christmas card and a letter to Dad now and again. He'd bought a sheep farm. Seemed to have done well. Never married. Since Dad died I've never heard from him and now POW! out of the blue. I am his only living relative so everything comes to me."

In the blank silence that followed Mr

Lorimer's words, Sally searched in her pocket, found the crystal unicorn and squeezed it tightly in her hand. She was almost afraid of it. To have worked such magic in a week. If they really had inherited a lot of money it made a pony of her own not only possible but almost certain.

"Do you perhaps think . . ." she began at exactly the same moment as Ben started to say something about bookcases but it was Mrs Lorimer who spoke first.

"Kestrels?" she said.

"Why not?" said Mr Lorimer and he put his hand in his pocket and brought out three keys on a ring attached to a label. "Thought one of you might suggest it so I popped into the estate agent's and got the keys."

Suddenly everyone was talking and laughing, all at the same time, while the Beardies leapt about in mad, Chinese-dragon cascades of hair.

"Can we go to Kestrels now?" Em asked.

"I'll make up a picnic," said Mrs Lorimer, bouncing Jamie on her knee and telling him that they were going to live in a castle.

"Will there be dungeons?" he asked. "Dragons?"

"Well, cellars," said his mother. "And most definitely frogs."

"Not the day for fish paste sandwiches," said Mr Lorimer. "We'll stop at the supermarket and you can each fill a basket with whatever you like."

When they had all filled their baskets Mr Lorimer picked a bottle of champagne from the shelf.

"No glasses," said Ben so they went into a chemist and bought paper cups.

"We've come into a fortune," Sally told the assistant because she had to tell someone.

"Pigs might fly," said the girl, not even smiling and Sally saw pigs all colours of the rainbow flying lumpily about the sky. Pigs that changed into ponies, ponies that galloped and reared and flung up their heels into the air as if the whole sky were a daisy meadow.

"We can drive right up to the house, now it's ours," said Sally when they reached Kestrels. "Our house."

"Don't count your peacocks," said Mrs Lorimer. "It may be in such a terrible condition that we won't be able to consider buying it."

"That's not what the man at the estate

agent's said. He's coming down in the afternoon to show us round."

Meg and Misty had their heads out of the car window. Sally pushed them out of the way to get a better view. The grey tower of Kestrels with its paved forecourt and guardian stone dogs was waiting for them. She glanced back along the avenue and saw it was pitted with hoofprints.

Had the girl on her roan pony made them? Sally wondered. Perhaps she rode there a lot. And Sally realized that when, not *if* but *when*, they came to live at Kestrels she was bound to get to know the girl and her roan pony. Know their names. Even ride with them when she had her own pony.

They all stood grouped around Mr Lorimer as he unlocked the door. It groaned open and they were looking into a huge hallway. A wide wooden staircase flowed down towards them. Each of its newel posts was topped with a little hawk carved in wood.

"Kestrels," said Mr Lorimer as they walked through the doorway for the first time. Sally's family paused at the foot of the staircase admiring the carvings but Sally ran on, light foot, stirring the carpet of dust from the wooden stairs. At the very top of the stairs, hanging from an almost invisible wire was a hovering Kestrel, its wings outspread.

"Bet he loved them," said Mr Lorimer, catching up with Sally. "The man who carved them. They're almost alive."

"Is that the trap door to the tower?" Ben asked, pointing upwards.

"Could be," agreed Mr Lorimer and he lifted Sally onto his shoulders.

She could just reach the trap door, just enough to push it open. When the clouds of dust had settled she could see a stair spiralling upwards to a platform at the top of the tower. Some of the steps of the stair had fallen away, others clung on in rotting tatters of wood.

"No use," said Sally. "You could never climb up it but it is the tower. I can see the sky."

"Looks terribly dangerous to me," said Mrs Lorimer, peering upwards. "From this moment on it is totally forbidden."

Sally let down the trap door with a bang and the dust clouds choked them.

"Quick," said Em. "To the summer house before we all suffocate."

"And starve," added Ben.

Seen from the summerhouse the sea flickered in dancing diamonds of light. They each found a place on the decaying window seats and began to unpack the picnic.

"First," said Mr Lorimer, "a toast."

They stood up, holding out their paper cups to be filled with champagne.

"To Great Uncle Nathan, wherever he is. May he know the joy he is giving us."

"Great Uncle Nathan," they chorused.

As Sally lifted the cup to her lips, tasting the not-sweet taste and bubbles of the champagne, a goose walked over her grave. Shuddering, she suddenly knew that this was all for real. They really were coming to live here. She and Em would need to change schools. She might never ride at Miss Meek's again. They were all going to leave the house where Sally had always lived. The pony she had dreamed about for so long was going to change from a make-believe pony into a real live pony. And she would be responsible for it. There would be no Miss Meek keeping an eye on things.

Suddenly she wasn't hungry. Even her bag of goodies didn't tempt her. She ate some salmon pâté to stop her mother going on at her and then she stood up.

"I'm going for a walk," she said, hoping desperately that no one would offer to come with her. But no one did. They were all too busy eating; too busy talking. Even Meg and Misty did no more than roll their eyes at her, hardly daring to look away from the food.

Sally walked towards Kestrels, finding her way to the stables. After their first discovery of the stables the Lorimers had kept away from the house and outbuildings, feeling that there was more trespass involved if they prowled around the house than if they just wandered round the grounds.

Sally stopped at the entrance to the stable-yard. She stared around at the looseboxes and the buildings that must once have been feed-houses and tackrooms. As if in a dream she walked forward and looked into the first empty box and then the next. The stone floors were covered with dirt and dust and the walls festooned with dense cobwebs.

Sally crossed to the other side of the yard. She looked in through a door that was half-open and there, terrifying as Dracula in a horror film because it was so totally unexpected, were four bales of hay and an open bin half-full of pony nuts. On the wall hung polished tack. It was all exactly as Sally imagined it would be when she was keeping her own pony there. Sally clenched her eyes shut. Opened them again but nothing had changed. She swung round, ready to dash back to the summerhouse and tell her parents what she had found, when a trumpeting whinny ripped the air. There was a sound of hooves on stone and a roan pony head with prick ears and glistening eyes was trying to see over one of the box doors. The pony crashed his front hooves against the door and whinnied again.

"Tarquin! Behave yourself!" and coming into the yard, carrying a bucket of water, was the girl with the sunburst of golden hair; the roan pony's rider.

Chapter Five

The two girls stared at each other in amazement. Sally couldn't imagine what the girl was doing stabling her pony at Kestrels, but it didn't seem very right. She was about to say hallo when the girl spoke.

"You're trespassing," she said. "This is private property. You shouldn't be here."

Although the girl's voice sounded bossy Sally thought her eyes looked guilty.

"You'd better go home," the girl was saying when they both heard a man's footsteps coming towards the yard. "Who's that?" she asked, "someone with you?"

Sally shook her head. She knew it wasn't

her father. In an instant the girl had dashed across the yard and slammed the door shut on the hay and oats. She was just in time for a second later a middle-aged man wearing a smart suit and city shoes walked into the yard.

"Afternoon," he said. "I heard your voices. You'll be part of the Lorimer family, I expect."

Sally nodded.

"I'm Mr Scott from the estate agents," he was saying as he came across the yard towards them, when suddenly Tarquin neighed his impatience and clattered his hooves against the door.

"Blimey," said Mr Scott, turning pink with shock. "Is that a horse? Don't tell me you've brought a horse with you!"

Mr Scott marched past the girls and stared into the loosebox. "Well you seem to have made yourself at home," he said. "Moved in have you?"

The roan pony was standing on a thin bed of straw. Straw from last night's bed was piled at the sides of the box. An almost empty haynet hung by the side of the manger.

"Your father doesn't own the place yet, you know. Actually, you have absolutely no right to do this sort of thing."

The girl was staring down at her shoes, twisting her hands.

"We rode over," said Sally quickly.

"Well make sure and clear up before you ride back. Now where's your father?"

"They're in the summerhouse," said Sally. Mr Scott, with a last irritated glare at the pony, hurried out of the yard.

"Glory gosh," said the girl. "That was a close shave. Thanks for covering up. I couldn't think what to say. In another minute I'd have been telling him everything."

"What is everything?"

"Wait till I put the bucket in to Tarquin and then I'll explain."

The roan pony ruffled his muzzle through the water but didn't drink.

"Typical," said the girl.

"He's a super pony," said Sally, gazing in admiration, for Tarquin was as finely bred as a race horse. His arched neck held aloft a fine-boned silken-skinned head with lustrous eyes, neat ears curved like shells and a delicate muzzle. His mane was pulled to a light fringe and his tail fell in a neat tassle to just below his straight hocks. His smooth, iron-boned legs ended in small black hooves. He was completely different to any of Miss Meek's ponies. Totally and completely different to anything Sally had ever ridden.

"He is smashing. You are lucky," Sally said and was about to add how much she wanted her own pony but there wasn't much hope, when she suddenly remembered that it wasn't true any longer.

"I'm Thalia Nisbet. 'Thalia-rhymes-with-dahlia-which-is-a-flower-like-a-chrysanthemum.' "

"Oh," said Sally. "Well I'm Sally Lorimer. My whole family's here. We're going to buy Kestrels."

"Whee! What's your dad like? Will he let me go on keeping Tarquin here or is he going to use all the stables for his racehorses? I couldn't possibly have left Tarquin outside all winter. He'd have frozen to death. I've only ever used this one box. The hay and everything else is all mine. I delivered papers and walked dogs and I don't care what anyone says I haven't done any harm."

"Didn't anybody know?"

"Only my grandmother. I live with her. In a cottage just along the shore. No one else. They all thought I kept Tarquin in a field behind Narg's house. That's Gran spelt backwards because when my mum had me Narg said she wasn't going to be a grandmother but she would be a Narg, that would suit her better."

As she spoke Thalia's hazel eyes shone with excitement. She pushed her bony hands through her hair and chattered on as if she had known Sally all her life.

"But I will be putting him out in the field during the day now that the weather is getting better. He's a present from Mum and Dad. When they split up they gave me Tarquin. Of course I'd always wanted a pony and I'd always spent a lot of time at Narg's but all the same it was a bit weird – shattering my life and giving me a pony. When I asked them who had given me which end they couldn't even agree on that, so the off side is from my dad and the near side is from my mum."

"He looks really fast," said Sally.

"Oh he is. Do you want a ride? I'm just going out."

"Wouldn't you mind? Really? I'll need to tell Mum but I'll run."

"Perhaps you could say to your dad? About me?"

"He won't mind a bit," Sally assured her, as she turned and ran out of the stableyard, taking great leaps over the long grass. A French window was standing open and as Sally raced up the three cracked, uneven steps she could hear voices coming from the corridor beyond the drawing room.

Her family and Mr Scott were standing in a huge kitchen.

Sally pulled at her mother's arm.

"I've met a friend," she said. "She's the girl on the roan pony. Can I go for a ride with her?"

"Don't you want to see round the house. We couldn't find you."

"Mum, it's a pony."

"Well be careful," said her mother. "Be sure to borrow her hard hat."

When Sally got back to the yard Thalia had tacked up Tarquin and was standing outside waiting for her.

"Okay?"

"I've got to borrow your hat."

"It's soft as a pancake but you can have a shot of it if you want. Did you ask?"

"Hadn't a chance. But he won't mind. Honest."

"Hope so," said Thalia. "Do you want to ride first? We can go down the track to the shore and ride on the sands."

Now Tarquin was standing in the yard he looked twice the height he had been in his box. Thalia was holding him by the length of his reins as he pranced sideways, clinking his bit impatiently and kicking up his heels.

Sally regarded him nervously. "If Thalia let go of his reins he would gallop out of sight," she thought. She had seen ponies on television behaving like this but even at their local show the ponies usually plodded along quite calmly. But Tarquin wasn't like them. He was fire and lightning and she was going to have to ride him.

"Perhaps you'd better go first," Sally said. "I don't know the way down to the sands."

"Right," said Thalia, taking Tarquin's reins over his head, checking his girth and pulling down his stirrups. "He is pretty fresh."

Effortlessly her long legs swung her into the saddle. "This way," she said, riding out of the yard.

The door where Thalia kept her feed was

now securely locked. If Sally's parents and the estate agent came into the stableyard they would only see the bed in Tarquin's box. They would think it was only being used today.

Tarquin trotted down the narrow path to the shore.

"Tide's going out," said Thalia. "I usually school for a bit first. Then your turn, okay?"

Ignoring Tarquin's switching tail and shaking head Thalia rode him firmly away from Sally and began to walk him in a wide circle. Gradually the pony stopped messing about and began to pay attention to his rider, walking out with a long, reaching stride. Thalia squeezed her legs against his sides and he changed smoothly into a slow, sitting trot.

Watching, Sally knew that Thalia could really ride. In a few minutes she had changed a restive, unwilling pony into a calm, obedient one.

"I'll never be able to ride as well as that," Sally thought as she stared entranced at Tarquin and his rider silhouetted against the brightness of the sea. "Never."

"Right," said Thalia, walking Tarquin back to Sally. "Your turn."

Sally put on Thalia's hat which sank down over her ears like a tea cosy.

"Have you ridden quite a lot?" Thalia asked as Sally climbed into the saddle. In her excitement she had forgotten to put the toe of her shoe against the girth and had poked Tarquin in the ribs, making him leap sideways.

"At Miss Meek's riding school," said Sally, shortening her stirrups and thinking fondly of the riding school ponies who always stood like blocks of wood while riding crops flapped about their faces and new jodh boots gouged into their sides.

"Take him along the sands," said Thalia, letting go of Tarquin's bridle. "Give him a canter."

Sally gathered up her reins as she always did on Miss Meek's ponies. Tarquin threw up his head and broke into a ragged trot.

"Careful with his mouth," Thalia shouted. "Don't hang onto him like that."

But her warning was too late. Feeling the unbalanced rider on his back Tarquin trotted faster and faster.

"Steady, steady," Sally said. "Whoa now."

Tarquin seemed so narrow between her

knees. His neck reached upward, pointing his head at the sky so that Sally could see the whites of his eyes. She tried to change her reins into one hand so that she could clap his neck but they were a bulky muddle of leather which she couldn't sort out.

By now Tarquin was trotting faster than ever, far faster than a canter, the sand spurting from his hooves as if he were a Welsh trotting pony.

"Steady! Whoa!" pleaded Sally. "Stop! Oh please stop!"

Helplessly she bumped up and down on his hard, fit back, not even able to post, hardly able to stay in the saddle.

In front of them was a rotted breakwater. Tarquin pricked his sharp ears and thundered towards it.

"No!" screamed Sally, not caring who heard her. "Stop, Tarquin. Stop!" but Tarquin thundered on.

He leapt straight up into the air, straight over and straight down again. Sally flew up out of the saddle and thumped down on his neck at the other side. As she struggled back into the saddle, Tarquin swung round on his hocks, battered round the end of the breakwater, then, as if a rocket had blasted him from behind, he charged into a full gallop, his head low, his legs going like pistons.

Sally, clutching reins and the pommel of the saddle, clung on helplessly. The tiny figure of Thalia seemed miles away. As Tarquin raced towards her, Sally saw her family coming across the sand to join Thalia.

"Don't come off, don't come off," Sally told herself. "They'll never buy you a pony if they see you fall off."

Sally was completely out of control. There was nothing she could do to slow Tarquin down. If he wanted to gallop all the way back to the stables there was nothing Sally could do to stop him. She could only cling, tight with terror.

But when they reached Thalia Tarquin's gallop slowed to a canter. He stopped with three unseating bounces, making Sally clutch at handfuls of mane to stay on top. Sally waited expecting everyone to start asking her what had gone wrong, but to her amazement no one was paying much attention to her. Thalia and her father were talking about stabling, Mr Lorimer arranging to see Thalia's grandmother. Mrs Lorimer was holding Meg and Misty, trying to stop them digging in the sands, while Em, Ben and Jamie were grubbing about looking for shells and things.

"He loves a gallop," said Thalia. "I sometimes gallop the whole length of the beach. Did he behave?"

"And you can keep him in the field in the summer. We'll be fencing it in for Sally's pony," continued Mr Lorimer.

Sally slid down from Tarquin's back. She stood leaning against the pony, clutching his saddle to stop herself collapsing onto the sand.

She heard her father say, "Sally's pony," words she had longed to hear for many years. Her own pony. Sally's pony. But now she could do nothing but try to control her shaking arms, try to stop her legs trembling and wipe the tears off her face before anyone noticed.

"I'll pop in and see your Gran, sorry, Narg. Fix things up."

Thalia's thanks frothed out of her.

"When the firing squad has you lined up, send for me and I'll take your place," she promised Mr Lorimer and offered Sally another ride.

Sally swallowed hard but her mother spoke for her.

"Another time," she said to Thalia. "We didn't know we were coming here until this morning. It's the Parents' Association supper tonight so we've got to get back. But you'll have lots of time to get to know each other now that we're coming to be your new neighbours."

As they drove home to their house that wasn't home any longer Sally sat in the back of the car, clutching an unwilling Misty on her knee. She was squashed in by Em and Ben, and listened to her family talking excitedly at the top of their voices about all the things that they would do when they came to live at Kestrels. But she couldn't find a voice to join in.

Sally was still filled with the panic that had seized her when Tarquin had run away with her. So easily she could have been thrown over his head to crash face down into the rotting wood and rusty iron of the breakwater. So easily she could have come off and, her foot jammed in a stirrup, been dragged along behind him; his hooves thundering about her head. Sally clutched Misty tighter ar buried her face in her comforting warmth.

But it wasn't until she was lying in bed that night that she faced up to the truth.

"Sally Lorimer," she told herself. "You didn't want to ride Tarquin again, did you? You were glad you had to go home, weren't you?"

"I'd never ridden a thoroughbred pony like that before," Sally thought, making excuses for herself. "Never jumped like that before."

"You were afraid," said the voice in Sally's head, the voice that always spoke the truth. "Sally Lorimer you are nothing but a coward."

Chapter Six

The next fortnight was the most frantic, exciting time that Sally had ever known. Everything about her old life was vanishing. Soon there would be nothing of it left. Things that had lain in cupboards utterly undisturbed for years were crammed into black, polythene bags and thrown out. Plates and ornaments; pictures and books had all to be wrapped and packed into tea chests waiting for the removal men.

Mr Lorimer had sold their house to a fellow librarian who had just come up to Scotland from the south of England and wanted to move in before his wife and family joined him.

This meant they had to move into Kestrels as soon as possible.

Mrs Lorimer and several of her friends scrubbed and swept and vacuumed Kestrels while workmen carried out the most urgent repairs. Curtains and carpets were bought and fitted. Thalia's Narg, who was short and stout and charged about on a motor bike, set up a canteen in Kestrels' kitchen. She supplied everyone with soup, sandwiches and as much tea or coffee as they could drink.

"Most dear unknown Great Uncle Nathan," said Mr Lorimer. "We could never have afforded any of this without you. Thank you, thank you, thank you."

One evening, with the move only four days away, there was nothing really urgent that had to be done.

"I shall put my feet up and watch television," said Mrs Lorimer. "I am deprived of adverts."

"Seeing it's a nice evening, I thought Sally and I might take a walk over to the riding school?" suggested Mr Lorimer.

Sally looked up from learning her words. She hadn't been thinking about going to the riding school tonight. She had been planning to buy apples and carrots and say goodbye to the ponies on Friday afternoon, after her last day at school.

"I gave Miss Meek a ring at lunchtime so she'll be there tonight," said her father.

"Miss Meek is always there," said Sally.

"I mentioned to her that we were looking for a pony for you and she agreed that it would be a good idea to look at one of hers."

Sally's face grinned with utter surprise, her eyes opened wide with delight.

"You mean it?" she gasped. "You really mean it?"

"I tell you no lies. She suggested Clover as a possible pony. Said she was your favourite."

Sally skipped along beside her father and Em as they walked to the riding school.

"Pinch me," she kept saying to her sister. "Pinch me to make sure it's real."

She could not believe that her dream was coming true. So many times she had ridden up and down the lane on Clover imagining that the pony belonged to her and now . . .

Clover was standing tacked up in a loose-box. No one had bothered to give her a proper grooming. Her black coat was dull and her white socks were their usual shade of yellowish green. Even her long tail and straggling mane had not been brushed out.

When Miss Meek opened the box door Clover looked at them through weary, lack lustre eyes. She shifted her weight but made no attempt to walk towards them. Sally scratched her neck, spoke to her and gave her a sugar lump. Miss Meek freed the reins from Clover's stirrup and led her into the yard.

"Up you get," she said to Sally. "Ride her down the lane."

While Sally mounted, Clover stood like a wooden horse – head down, resting a hind leg.

"Wake her up," warned Miss Meek. "She's not used to being taken out alone."

Sally turned the unwilling pony towards the lane and tried to kick her on. But Clover, with a burst of sudden energy, swung round and would have carried Sally back into the box if Miss Meek hadn't caught her bridle.

"Varmit," she told the pony and led her to the beginning of the lane where she clapped Clover hard on the rump and sent her off at a ragged trot.

"Keep her going," she shouted at Sally.

"Don't let her get the better of you like that. Kick her on."

Obediently Sally kicked her heels into Clover's wooden sides.

"It's only Clover you're on," she told herself severely, "not Tarquin." For when Clover had tried to carry her back into the box Sally had felt her heart tighten with the same panic she had felt when Tarquin had run away with her.

Sally rode at Clover's slow walk to the end of the lane.

"What's wrong with you Sally Lorimer?" she asked herself. "Here you are riding your favourite pony and you're cross and narky and . . ." but Sally couldn't bring herself to add "scared" for what was there to be scared about when she was riding Clover? Scared in case Clover got out of control? Scared in case she ran away with her?

When they reached the end of the lane Clover turned, walked a few strides, trotted, and at exactly the place where the rides always cantered she broke into an uneven rocking-horse canter. She trotted again at exactly the place where the rides always slowed to a trot. Back at the beginning of the lane Clover suggested that they should return to the yard but Sally kicked and pulled at the reins and after a moment's struggle Clover gave in and plodded back down the lane.

After she had ridden up and down the lane a few times Sally rode back to the yard. When Clover was with the other riding school ponies Sally had enjoyed riding her but riding her alone wasn't the same at all. Clover would always expect to be hit and kicked; expect heavy hands to tug on her reins, jabbing her in the mouth; for that was the way she was always ridden. If she took Clover away from her lane Sally didn't think she would be able to control her at all.

In the yard Miss Meek was telling her father that Clover would make an ideal pony for his daughter; that owning a pony was not the same as riding at a riding school and that Clover, being perfectly reliable, would take good care of Sally.

"Well, how did she go for you?" asked Miss Meek, being briskly enthusiastic.

"Okay," said Sally. "Shall I take her tack off?"

"Put her in strip five," Miss Meek told Sally when she brought Clover out of the box.

Sally pulled the halter over Clover's ears and set her free. The pony waited to snatch Sally's offering of sugar lumps then swung away to tear at the short, over-grazed grass.

Sally blinked hard. For a miserable second she saw Clover grazing in the newly fenced field at Kestrels. Knew that she had only to say, yes she would love to have Clover, and that was what would happen. But she shook her head to clear the thought from her mind.

"Well then?" said Mr Lorimer in the tone of voice that showed that he thought everything was settled.

"No," said Sally, her throat so tight that she could hardly speak. "I don't want Clover. I'm sorry but I really don't want a riding school pony."

"Honestly," said Em as they walked home. "A month ago, if Dad had offered to buy Clover you would have been over the moon."

Sally scuffed her feet along the pavement. She couldn't find words to tell them that, much as she liked Clover, she didn't want a pony that was used to everyone riding it; used to kicks and jabs in the mouth. The pony she was looking for had to be special.

"Don't upset yourself," said her father. "Lots of time to look around."

Sally smiled up at him gratefully. She would find her pony the way she had found her unicorn.

Chapter Seven

They moved to Kestrels on a day of pouring rain – the removal men were bad tempered and the Beardies left wet, hairy footprints on the new carpets. Narg's soup kitchen was crowded out. Jamie sat under the table and ate a whole tin of chocolate biscuits.

The night before, Mrs Lorimer had said that they must make up their minds about bedrooms.

"Dad and I have picked ours in the corridor to the right and there's a smallish room next to us for Jamie. Now the rest of you?"

With one voice Ben, Em and Sally all said,

"The room at the top of the stairs."

"I'm the eldest," stated Ben, seeing himself sitting in the room at the top of the stairs surrounded by books.

"I'm the eldest *girl*," said Em. "And that's what matters. You have to be polite and let me have what I want."

"Ho, ho," said Ben.

"Fetch the straws," said Mr Lorimer.

Em brought three drinking straws. Mr Lorimer cut the end of one of them then held them out so that all the straws looked even. You could not tell which was the short one.

"Short straw," said Mr Lorimer. "Top room."

Em drew first. Sally shut her eyes. She couldn't even bear to watch.

"Bad luck," said Mrs Lorimer as Em drew a long straw.

"Now Sally."

"Oh I want it so badly," Sally said.

"Get on with it," said Ben. "Stop messing about. I'm bound to win."

Sally gave the two straws a last hard stare. One of them meant having the highest room in Kestrels for her own. She imagined herself sitting in the window seat, staring out over the wild winter sea or in the summer being able to see right along the shore line. Only from the top of the tower would there be a better view.

"Please, please," she whispered, and picturing her unicorn in her mind's eye she screwed her eyes shut again and grabbed one of the straws from her father's hand.

"Oh no!" exclaimed Ben. "Trust her. It's not fair."

And Sally knew that the top bedroom was hers.

On their first night at Kestrels Sally, sitting up in bed with Misty asleep at her feet, could see out across the water. She called to Starfire and he came cantering over the water, then faded from Sally's sight like the dream he was. Biddy and Lucia, trotting behind him, vanished too. Things were real now, their wish had come true.

That evening Sally had helped Thalia bed down Tarquin. Soon her own pony would be standing in the box next to him. Not a riding school pony nor an almost thoroughbred like Tarquin but her own pony. With an electric shock of amazement Sally realized that her own pony must be somewhere, at this very moment waiting for her to find it.

Sally closed her eyes, almost asleep, trying to imagine the pony that would be hers. At first she couldn't picture anything and then Tarquin was there and at once she was riding him. The sounds of his pounding hooves mingled with her own screams as he bolted over the shore. And again Sally felt the terrible panic of being totally helpless.

She started awake and lay trembling, afraid to go to sleep again in case the nightmare was waiting for her.

Ben and Mr Lorimer had to leave half an hour earlier in the morning to get to work and Sally and Em were going to a new school. It was a small three-teacher school. Knowing Thalia made it all quite easy. She seemed to be popular with all the children and introduced Em and Sally as her new friends.

"Well so you are," said Thalia when Sally tried to thank her. "But you'd be a better friend if you'd only hurry up and get a pony. I keep offering you rides on Tarquin but you won't."

"When I have my own pony we can ride together."

"But *when*. If only you'd keep on at your dad."

Sally kept on at her father and taking Thalia with them they went to see a pony that was advertised in the local paper as a super safety ride. It turned out to be a Shetland and far too small for Sally.

"I think," said Mr Lorimer as they drove away, "we need someone who knows about buying ponies. I shall ask Miss Wevell. She often arrives at the library in her jodhs, so I feel she must know about horses."

Miss Wevell was delighted to help. She knew a Mr Josh Frazer who had stables close to Kestrels. She said she would phone him up to see if he had any suitable ponies for sale and if he had she would come with them to give the ponies the once over.

When Thalia heard that they were going to Mr Frazer's stables she said at once that she was coming with them.

"It is *the* place," she said. "No one but the poshest of the posh goes there."

As they drove into Mr Frazer's yard the next Saturday Sally's heart sank. Thalia was right. It was the poshest. A range of smartly painted looseboxes surrounded by an immaculate stableyard. There was not a wisp of straw or hay to be seen anywhere. Miss Wevell, Thalia, Sally and Mr Lorimer got out of the car and appearing as if from thin air Mr Frazer was striding across the yard to greet them.

"Now then," he said when the introductions were over. "You're looking for a pony. Who is it for?"

"Sally, my daughter," said Mr Lorimer.

"Ah yes," said Mr Frazer. He had a long weatherbeaten face with flat cheeks and bright blue eyes. "So you want your own pony? How much riding have you done?"

"Only at a riding school," said Sally, feeling that to please Mr Frazer she should have ridden over the cross-country course at Badminton.

"A beginner?" asked Mr Frazer, turning to Mr Lorimer.

"I think we might say that," agreed her father smiling at Sally.

"Then I think I might have the very pony. Martine, bring out Bilbo, please."

A dark haired girl wearing a black jacket, jodhpurs and black boots went into one of the boxes. Sally was sure she had seen her somewhere before but it wasn't until she was leading a stocky bay pony towards them that Sally remembered where. She was the girl who had been in charge of the rides that Sally had seen when they picnicked at Fintry Bay. The horses must have come from these stables.

Bilbo had a hogged mane, a white star and a pink muzzle that pushed at Sally's pockets hoping for titbits.

Sally clapped his neck and told him that she hadn't anything for him, not liking to give him sugar lumps in front of Mr Frazer.

"Right. What do you think of him?" said Mr Frazer while Miss Wevell looked critically at the pony, running her hand down his sturdy legs and looking at his teeth in a knowledgeable way.

"Eight years old," said Mr Frazer. "Totally genuine child's pony. Bring any vet you like to look at him. He's perfectly sound. The boy who had him grew out of him. Bought his new pony from me and they asked me to sell Bilbo for them."

Thalia whispered to Sally that he didn't look very fast to her and could he jump and Mr Frazer asked Sally if she wanted to try him.

"Do you like him?" asked her father and Sally nodded, her heart thumping in her throat with excitement.

"Up you get then," said Mr Frazer and feeling that they were all watching her Sally was suddenly nervous; almost wished that it was Thalia who had to ride Bilbo.

Sally mounted and Mr Frazer led the way to a grass paddock. Bilbo walked round with a steady, workmanlike stride. When Sally asked him to trot he changed at once into a bouncy trot. When she had ridden him round in both directions Sally asked him to canter and he changed without any fuss, hardly increasing his speed. He did not feel a runaway type of pony at all.

"There you are," said Mr Frazer. "Goes well for you. No need to be nervous." Sally wondered how he knew.

"Need to try him on the road in traffic," said Miss Wevell, knowing all about horses.

"There's a ride going out in quarter of an hour," said Mr Frazer. "Sally can join them. Martine Dawes is taking the ride so she'll be in safe hands."

Sally rode at the front of the ride beside Martine Dawes who was riding her black horse. There were two teenage boys behind them and four women and a girl a bit older than Sally on a piebald pony.

The horses' hooves made a grand clatter on the flat shore road. Even when they trotted, Bilbo kept up easily with Martine's black horse. He looked about him with a bright, self-assured intelligence and when Sally spoke to him his black-tipped ears flickered back and forward at the sound of her voice.

"He's going well for you," said Martine. "Nice pony. He'd suit you."

Sally sat up straighter than ever, trying hard to remember all Miss Meek's instructions. She was just settling into enjoying herself when Martine stood up in her stirrups and looked back at her ride.

"We go down to the shore here," she called. "Keep in single file and space yourselves out. Charlotte, keep Pie back, keep him clear of Bracken's heels."

"Down to the sands," gasped Sally, suddenly realizing that of course she had always seen the ride on the beach.

"Yes," said Martine. "The horses love it. Gives them a good canter."

"But I don't want to ride on the sands," said Sally.

She felt the terror of her runaway ride on Tarquin tightening her throat and chest. She was sure that this time she would fall off, fall in amongst the galloping hooves of the horses.

"Oh please," she said. "I don't want to gallop," but Martine was shouting to one of the ladies to stop gossiping and pay attention to her horse.

"Down here," said Martine, leading the way down a steep track that led through the sand dunes and onto the beach.

"No!" screamed Sally inside her head. "I'm not! I'm not!"

But Bilbo was following the black horse with tight, springy strides. He had every intention of having a gallop.

All around Sally was a glistening brightness. The same glare of sea and sand as when Tarquin had run away with her and suddenly Sally wasn't sure who she was riding; to Sally's taut nerves the solid Bilbo might have been Tarquin.

The whole ride had reached the sands by now and Sally seemed surrounded by plunging horses.

"Steady," warned Martine. "Walk until I tell you to canter. Keep them under control."

"I'm not galloping," shrieked Sally. "Honestly, I'm not," her voice vanishing into a high squeak.

"Rubbish," exclaimed Martine, her attention on her ride. "Bilbo won't go fast."

"I'll wait here," said Sally desperately, and she tried to turn the bay pony back to the track.

At the same moment Martine touched her black horse into a slow, controlled canter, keeping her ride behind her.

Sally tightened her reins, pulling wildly at Bilbo's mouth. The pony fought to follow the others and Sally knew she couldn't hold him. The only thing she could do was to get off. In a blind panic she kicked one foot free of her stirrup just as Bilbo tucked down his head and bucked, then went charging after the ride.

At once Martine was calling to the ride to stop as she swung her black horse round and came cantering back to Sally. Bilbo ducked and swerved past her with Sally clinging to the saddle, her mind a blank blur of fear.

Bilbo reached the ride who were straggled out across the sands – some slowed to a walk, the two boys still cantering. Sally felt herself slipping, caught a vivid glimpse of Bilbo's shoulder, then the wet sand slapped her with a stinging blow on the side of her face. For seconds Sally lay there, the sand against her eye, then she was scrambling to her feet telling everyone that she was all right.

Once they had made sure that Sally really wasn't hurt and Bilbo had come trotting back to investigate the happening, Martine took a leading rein out of her pocket.

"I had no idea you were trying to stop him," she said – cross with Sally, cross with herself. "Up you get. I'll put a rein on him until we reach the road."

"No. I'm not getting on again. I'm not. I'm not."

"Lead him back to the road then."

"No. I'm not riding again."

Sally was almost surprised at what she was saying. She listened to her voice repeating over and over again that she was not riding.

It took some time to sort out what they

were going to do but in the end the girl on the piebald waited with Sally while the ride – Martine leading Bilbo – went back to the stables to tell Mr Lorimer that his daughter was waiting to be picked up.

"You should have got on again," said the girl on the piebald scornfully. "You should always get on again after a fall."

Now that it was all over, Sally knew that she had made a total fool of herself. Bilbo wouldn't have run away with her. She had often cantered on Clover at the riding school. It was the memory of Tarquin's galloping that had filled her with such fear.

"I'm going to school for a bit," said the girl on the piebald. "Let me know when your father arrives," and she rode away to firmer sand.

Sally went up to wait in the sand dunes by the side of the road, feeling completely miserable.

As she watched for their car a ramshackle, falling-to-bits horsebox rattled slowly past. A dapple grey pony looked out from between the slats. In the second that it was driven past it looked straight at her and Sally knew she had found her pony.

As Sally gazed after the horse box, their car drew up beside her.

"Do you know that horse box?" Sally demanded, grabbing open the back door of the car, almost pulling Thalia out.

"There, that one."

"It's Jas. Turnball's. I hate him. He collects old ponies, takes them to sales in England and then you know what happens to them," and Thalia spat violently into the gutter making Miss Wevell tut and Mr Lorimer raise his eyebrows in mild surprise.

Chapter Eight

It seemed a long drive back to Kestrels. Once her father had made sure that Sally hadn't hurt herself he started talking to Miss Wevell about the books needed for a new branch library. Sally stared out of the window, her arms folded, her shoulders hunched. Thalia tried unsuccessfully to discover exactly what had happened but soon gave up trying.

"But you could have ridden on the road again?" asked her mother when she had heard their story.

"I didn't want to," stated Sally. "I just didn't want to ride again."

Now that she was safely home the common

sense part of Sally hardly knew why she hadn't taken Bilbo up to the road and ridden back with the ride. But the hidden, dark part of Sally knew that she would never gallop again. She still wanted a pony as badly as ever; wanted the grey pony so much that she was sure she would find some way of rescuing it and bringing it to Kestrels. But she was never, ever going to gallop again.

It did not seem a good time to mention the grey pony to her family so Sally decided that she would need to find it herself. When she had eaten enough salad and quiche to satisfy her mother Sally went down to the stables hoping to find Thalia there. Jamie and the dogs went too.

"I'm only going to the stables to find Thalia," Sally told Jamie, not wanting to be bothered with him. "You'll get bored."

"I'll find mice," said Jamie. "For Em."

"You will not. You know she hates them."

"She'll scream," said Jamie happily.

Thalia was cleaning tack. Tarquin was in the field.

"Thought you might have had a nervous crash-down," said Thalia.

"Well I didn't," said Sally. "All this fuss

because I didn't want to gallop."

"Bilbo didn't look to me as if he could gallop," said Thalia, polishing her saddle. "If you hadn't been so daft you could have had Bilbo here, now. We could have been riding together. I think you've changed your mind. You don't want a pony."

"I do and I know which pony I want. You'll see."

"Well you'd better be quick. It's the summer holidays in three weeks and then in two weeks it's the gymkhana. You'd better have your pony for that!"

Sally ignored the thought of the gymkhana. She wasn't interested in it. It was bound to mean galloping.

"You know Mr Turnball – we saw his horse box? Where does he live?"

Thalia looked up in surprise at the urgency in Sally's voice.

"Why do you want to know?" she demanded.

"There was a grey pony . . ." Sally began.

"Well don't go hanging around there," warned Thalia. "It just breaks your heart, that's all it does. He buys old ponies and his mate drives them down south to pony sales. Then they're meat. And you can't stop them because it's legal. And I hate him and I hate everyone who sells their ponies to him. So I'm telling you, keep away."

"Where does he live?" Sally repeated. She had been hoping that Thalia would help her save the grey pony but obviously Thalia wasn't going to become involved with Mr Turnball.

"You know the farm with the pink walls. You can see it across the fields from the school bus. If you go back towards Fintry Bay there's a stile with a sign post and a right of way."

"Oh yes," said Sally, remembering the sign post. "It says 'Craigbet'?"

"That's right. But don't go near him. He's foul. The whole place is utterly foul," and Thalia spat onto the stone floor.

"You shouldn't spit. It's pooh," said Jamie smugly, "I've found one," and he held out his plump hand showing them the soft body of a dead vole.

"That's much worse than spitting," said Sally. "Go and bury it."

But seeing that his sister wasn't really too worried about his find Jamie tucked it into his pocket.

Suddenly Meg and Misty exploded into barking that changed to leaping and wagging as Sally's parents came into the yard.

"So this is where you are?" said Sally's mother.

"Look," said Jamie, pulling the vole out of his pocket.

"Throw it away. Now. At once," commanded Mrs Lorimer.

"I've been telling Sally that she won't have a pony for the gymkhana if she doesn't get a move on," said Thalia.

"I will," said Sally. "You'll see I will. *If* I want to go to the gymkhana I'll have a pony to ride."

Sally tossed and turned all night. She could think of nothing except the grey pony. At half-past five she got up. Looking out of her window the sea was a polished metal lake and the sky a high dome of dull silver. She took the unicorn from its place on the window ledge and slipped it into her jeans' pocket. She would need it to help her find the grey pony.

She took biscuits from the tin for herself, two slices of bread and a sliced carrot for the pony and clipped on Misty's lead knowing she would bark if she was left behind. She collected Tarquin's halter from its nail by his box. Tarquin, asleep in the straw, didn't even open an eye. She jumped her way down the path to the shore and ran along the sands watching the other side of the road for the signpost to Craigbet.

It was further than Sally had remembered but at last she saw it. She climbed over the sand dunes, across the road, over the stile and at a jog trot followed the right of way through the fields.

By the time she saw the pink-washed farm house in the distance her watch said twenty-five to seven. Soon her family would be waking up and wondering where she was.

"They'll think I've taken you for a walk," she said to Misty who was dragging behind, fed up with being on her lead. But Sally knew that in another half hour they would really start looking for her. She shouldn't be taking Misty for a walk, she should be getting ready for school. She couldn't think how it had taken her so long.

She ran on until she was close to the farm then stopped. There didn't seem much point in knocking on Mr Turnball's door. Sally did not think he would be pleased to see her.

"Now keep close to me," she told Misty, tugging at her lead. "And keep quiet. Don't dare bark."

Sally crept down the side of a hawthorn hedge, her trainers filling with muddy water. Half-way down the hedge cattle were grazing but there were no ponies with them. As Sally passed them the cows stopped grazing and followed her down their side of the fence. At the end of the hedge they waited in the corner of the field watching through long-lashed eyes as Sally climbed over a gate.

Misty made a half-hearted attempt to squeeze through the bars. When Sally tried to pull her through she lay on her back, paws flopping, eyes rolling.

"It's a good job you're not Meg," said Sally as she hoisted her over the gate. "I could never have lifted Meg over. Now come on."

A stream meandered down one side of the field, turning to the right and hidden from Sally's sight by clustering willow trees; but even from the top of the gate Sally had not seen any sign of ponies.

"When I saw the grey pony, Mr Turnball might have been taking it away," she thought suddenly. "Not bringing it here at all. But it must be here. It must."

Sally knew that if the grey pony had been driven south she would never see it again.

"Don't think about it," she told herself. "Your pony's here," and she started to run down the side of the stream. Glancing at her watch she saw it was almost ten to seven. They would all be really worried about her by now, but she didn't care. She was not going home until she had found her pony.

She ran round the turn of the stream and there on the flat ground were six ponies. Sally stopped block still. There were three browns, two bays and a chestnut, all old and weary. But no grey pony. Tears of disappointment filled Sally's eyes. Where would she look now? Then she saw a movement in the clump of willows at the side of the stream.

Under the green shadows of the weeping willows the grey pony was standing alone, watching Sally.

"Oh pony!" cried Sally and she could only stand and wait as the pony walked slowly towards her, her wide nostrils trembling with a silent whinnying welcome.

The pony was about 13.2 hands high. A

dapple grey mare, her ribs showing through her harsh coat; her neck sunken, her quarters flat. Her long white mane and tail drifted as she walked. She had an Araby dished face and huge Arab eyes. As she walked towards Sally she dragged her near hind leg and Sally saw it was torn from the point of her quarters to below her hock.

Sally pushed her hand under the pony's long mane, stroked her neck and ran her hand over the bony shoulders, telling the pony that she loved her.

"Dad will buy you for me," Sally whispered. "We'll come for you tonight."

Cautiously she took the carrot strips out of her pocket, offering them secretly to the pony so that the other ponies wouldn't see.

Very gently the grey pony took the slice of carrot from Sally's hand. Sheer happiness filled Sally's whole being.

"You'll love Kestrels," she told the grey pony when suddenly Misty plunged forward, splitting the silence with her barking.

Sally looked up from the pony to see a small, dark-haired man walking towards her. He was wearing heavy rubber boots, soiled jeans and a filthy tweed jacket. His face was dark with unshaved beard and his beady eyes were fixed on Sally.

"And what do you think you're up to?" he demanded, walking closer to Sally.

Misty lifted her lips, revealing pink gums and crocodile teeth. She snarled from the depths of her throat. The man stood still.

"I came to see the grey pony," said Sally.

"Thought my farm was a public park, eh?"

"I want to buy her," said Sally, her voice sounding shaky.

"Do you now? Well I dare say that could be arranged. I'm in the business of selling horse flesh. You'll need to be hasty. I've come to get them in. Two hours from now and this little lot will all be off on their summer holidays."

Sally kept her arm over the grey pony's withers. Her other hand clutched tightly onto Misty's lead. As long as she had Misty she felt sure the man, who she supposed was Mr Turnball, wouldn't come any closer.

"Please keep the grey pony," she pleaded. "Don't send her away with the others. Dad will pay for her tonight. Honestly he will. You must keep her for me."

"I'd have my fields full of little ponies waiting for the likes of you to bring me their money. You want her, you have the cash in my hand before ten this morning or she'll have gone with the rest. Now get off with you."

Sally swung blindly away. The stream flowed over pebbles and, dragging Misty behind her, she ran across it and went full pelt across the fields in the direction of Kestrels. Not keeping to paths or stiles she raced furiously on.

It was almost twenty-five past seven on her watch. Her father and Ben left the house at around a quarter to eight. Her only hope of saving the grey pony was to catch her father and persuade him to come to Mr Turnball's now. It was no use asking her mother. She would only say, Wait until your father comes home, and by then it would be too late.

Misty stopped at a sudden smell, pulling her collar over her head but Sally hardly paused. Every second was vital. She stuffed Misty's collar and lead into her pocket, felt her forgotten unicorn, and grasping it in her hand she ran desperately on, hoping to reach the road to Kestrels' gates before her father.

At last she saw the grey strip of road, the marram grass, the washed line of the sea. Her breath burnt in her lungs, her legs staggered as she forced herself to keep going.

It was almost a quarter to eight when the gates of Kestrels came into sight. Only a field of rough grazing, spiked with gorse bushes, lay between her and home. Staring at the open, rusted gates Sally ran mechanically on, knowing that it was always possible that her father and Ben had gone. That she was already too late.

Their car came down the avenue as Sally was half-way across the field.

"Stop!" she screamed. "Stop. Dad stop!"

Sally raced madly to the road, yelling her loudest and waving her arms above her head. Her foot caught on the root of a gorse bush and she fell flat on the ground.

At the gates of Kestrels Mr Lorimer paused to check the road and, turning right, drove off to Tarent.

By the time Sally had scrambled to her feet the car was out of sight.

Chapter Nine

Sally ran on blindly, running as if there was still hope; as if she had only seen the car in her imagination. She climbed over the stone wall, crossed the road and stood in Kestrels' gateway, tears running down her face, not knowing what she was going to do now.

A car swung into the drive, swerved to avoid Sally then skidded to a halt.

"Sally!" roared her father as he burst out of the car. "What on earth are you doing here?"

Sally stared unbelievingly, then flung herself into her father's arms, sobbing out her story.

"So please, she is the pony I want. She is

the pony I would like. Please come back now, at once, or she'll have gone. He said we must be there before ten."

"Steady on," said Mr Lorimer, offering Sally his handkerchief. "Here, mop up. I'd be well on my way to work by now if it hadn't been for Misty."

Blowing her nose, Sally looked at the car and realized that Misty was sitting in the back seat. Ben was gripping her ruff, his attention on his book.

"She got away from me."

"We found her sniffing along the road. Caught her and turned to bring her back. So it's Misty you've to thank. Now, get in and let's see what we can do. You are sure this is the pony you want?"

"Really sure," affirmed Sally when she was established in the back seat beside Misty. "More than wanting the dentist to stop drilling."

"If you really are certain," said her father. Ben said it was only double gym so it didn't matter if he was a bit late.

Mr Lorimer drove to Craigbet farm. He told Sally to stay where she was and crossed the littered yard to knock on the farm door.

Sally could hardly believe what was happening. It had all changed so suddenly from total despair to the hope that in a few minutes the grey pony would be hers.

Mr Turnball came to the door, spoke with her father, then they walked across the yard together and Mr Turnball pushed open a barn door. He went in and came out leading the grey pony by a coarse rope round her neck.

"Is this the one?" asked Mr Lorimer.

"Yes," said Sally, getting out of the car and the grey pony turned her delicate, wild-flower face and riffled her nostrils, knowing Sally.

"Right," said her father. "You have chosen," and he took out his cheque book.

Mr Turnball chucked the rope in Sally's direction as he scuttled to Mr Lorimer's side to discuss the price. Sally fitted Tarquin's halter round the grey pony's head and knotted it securely, telling the pony that she was safe now.

"Pleasure to do business with you," smarmed Mr Turnball as her father told Sally that if she could lead the pony he would drive slowly in front of her.

The car bumped over the potholes of the

farm road and Sally walked beside her pony, for this short time completely happy, wanting nothing else in the whole world.

Mr Lorimer went slowly on along the road, turned down the avenue and drove to Kestrels. Hearing the car Mrs Lorimer, Jamie and Meg came rushing out. The grey pony stood at Sally's side looking about her with mild interest. She didn't even flinch when the Beardies bounded around her.

"Where have you been?" demanded her mother. "I've been so worried about you."

Sally and Mr Lorimer explained.

"You should have left a note," stated Mrs Lorimer. "No, I'm not listening to any excuses. And what about school? Em's away without you."

"Yes," said Ben from the car. "I don't mind missing gym but I've got to be there for Social Studies."

"Right, we're off," said Mr Lorimer and they drove away.

"The poor pony's got a sorely leg," said Jamie. "It's all bleeding."

Guiltily Sally remembered her pony's leg.

"She wasn't lame when I was leading her," she said hurriedly.

"Looks nasty to me," said her mother. "I'll phone the vet."

"And school? I don't need to go today do I?"

Mrs Lorimer hugged her daughter to her. "Well," she said. "For this once."

"Does she look very old?" said Sally anxiously.

"Well . . . thin," said her mother. "Tired too. Whatever made you pick her?"

"Love," said Sally.

When Mr Cheever, the vet, arrived, he was young with longish hair, purple jeans and a gaudy tee shirt. He said the cut wasn't deep and fortunately not septic. He gave the grey pony two injections which made Sally curl her toes, but didn't seem to bother the pony at all.

"Is she very old?" asked Sally, deciding it was better to know than go on worrying about it.

"Old?" said the vet. "Oh, six, seven."

A grin of relief spread across Sally's face.

"She's in poor condition but nothing that a few weeks of good feeding won't sort out. You've got a very nice pony. Welsh mountain type. You'll be riding her in a week or two. Be seeing you at the gymkhana? I'm the official vet."

Sally wanted to say, no, she didn't think she would be at the gymkhana but the vet had turned to Mrs Lorimer and was talking to her about feed and the best place to buy it.

"Right," he said, packing up his bag and pushing Misty away. "I'll pop in tomorrow, give her another injection. Keep her in until I see her again."

"Thank you for coming," said Sally as the vet and her mother went back to Kestrels.

Sally laid her arms along the top of the half door, resting her chin on her hands. In her mind's eye she saw the pony standing watching her from under the willow trees.

"Willow," said Sally. "That's your name. Willow," and the grey pony turned to look inquiringly at Sally, almost as if she knew her name.

Thalia came straight from school.

"What a super pony!" she exclaimed. "Super! I thought you didn't want a fast pony. When she's fit she'll be as fast as Tarquin. Now! You stop being so nervous and we can have the most super best summer. We can jump and gallop and ride over to the Tarent Show and we can go in for the pairs jumping at the cross-country . . ."

Thalia's face was alight with enthusiasm but Sally turned quickly away. She felt fear twist in the pit of her stomach, tighten her head. For a split second she was riding Tarquin again, being carried away in a helpless blur of terror.

"The vet doesn't know when she'll be fit to ride."

"Four weeks to the gymkhana," said Thalia. "She'll be fit for the games."

The vet came again the next day. He gave Willow another injection and said she could go out during the day; that the grass would be the best thing for her.

On Thursday evening he dropped in to check up on her. Sally had tied Willow to the gate post of the field and was brushing out her mane with a dandy brush while Thalia rode Tarquin in schooling circles at a sitting trot. Mr Lorimer, Jamie and the vet walked down to the field.

"Let's see the patient," said the vet, examining Willow's cut which had scabbed over. "Good. No heat at all and she's looking much better in herself. No reason why you shouldn't start riding her. Take it easy to begin with."

"Will Sally be able to ride her at the gymkhana?" Thalia asked the vet.

"Oh yes. No problem," said the vet and he turned to walk back to Kestrels, discussing with Mr Lorimer plans to landscape the grounds.

"There you are," triumphed Thalia. "You can come."

"Need to wait and see," said Sally, avoiding Thalia's direct stare.

They measured Willow for a saddle and bridle and on Sunday Miss Wevell drove up to Kestrels with the boot of her Mini stacked with tack borrowed from a friendly saddler.

Willow stood patiently in her box while Miss Wavell fitted saddles and bridles. "There," she announced at last. "That's a nice broad snaffle and that saddle looks good to me. Up you get and we'll see what it's like with you on top."

"It's the first time Sally's ridden her," said Em, who was watching with the rest of her family and Thalia.

"Take it easy then," said Miss Wevell and held Willow's bridle while Sally mounted. But the pony made no fuss. Miss Wevell squinted under the saddle to make sure it wasn't resting on Willow's spine, then she told Sally to ride her round the yard. Sally gathered up her reins, squeezed her legs against Willow's sides and she was riding her own pony.

Fizzy with happiness Sally rode down to the field and walked Willow round. The pony seemed as happy as Sally as she walked out with a long balanced stride. Sally asked her for a trot and she trotted out confidently, settling back to a walk the minute Sally asked her to.

"Go on," shouted Thalia. "Canter."

Sally walked Willow over to the gate.

"No," she said. "She's not fit to canter," and Miss Wevell told her to stand still while she checked the saddle again.

Sally got up very early the next morning and rode Willow in the field by herself. Willow walked quietly round, enjoying the early morning stillness with ears pricked and eyes bright.

"We'll just ride by ourselves to begin with," Sally told Willow, clapping her shoulder and leaning forward to press her cheek against her pony's neck.

Even when the holidays started Sally still rode by herself in the early mornings. During the day she helped Thalia to set up jumps for Tarquin or watched her schooling. Thalia, long-legged and totally sure that there was nothing Tarquin couldn't do, made it all look so easy.

"She would gallop and jump anything," Sally thought, watching enviously.

A week before the gymkhana Thalia appeared at Kestrels with the entry forms.

"These have to be filled in and posted today," she announced, plonking herself down on the stairs.

"I'm not going," said Sally. "I've told you."

"Well I'm entering you for the games," said Thalia, filling in the form. "Willow is perfectly fit. You're bound to change your mind."

But although Willow was beginning to look sleek and rounded, Sally did not change her mind. Even on the night before the gymkhana when she was sitting on the window seat in her bedroom, looking out over the long stretch of sands to the white tents of the gymkhana field in the distance, Sally knew that going to the gymkhana would mean galloping and she was never, every going to gallop again.

"You'd love to go," accused the voice in her head.

"I would not," Sally replied instantly. "I am never, ever going to gallop again. Not ever." And she held the crystal unicorn up to the dim evening light, a brightness in her hand.

Chapter Ten

Sally stood on the steps of Kestrels, her hands behind her back, her nails digging into her palms to stop herself crying.

"I'm sure. I'm quite sure. I don't want to come with you," she stated.

All her family, except Ben who was in Tarent, were sitting in the car. Meg was sitting on Em's knee panting. They were on their way to join Thalia at the gymkhana.

Sally had spent her morning trying to help Thalia get Tarquin ready for the gymkhana but Thalia had kept saying that it was quite all right, she could manage and if Sally wanted to groom a pony why didn't she groom Willow.

"We would all so much rather you came with us," said her mother. "But if you really don't want to come you can go on searching for Misty. Now don't do anything silly. We'll be back about five. Oh Sally, come on. Jump in."

"No," and Sally turned away quickly, going back into the house so that they wouldn't see her eyes filling with tears.

"Don't care," she thought. "The last thing I want to do is to ride at their rotten gymkhana. I'd rather ride here by myself. Much rather."

But all the time she was wishing that she had gone with Thalia, riding together to the gymkhana, Tarquin and Willow spruced and poshed up.

"But you're safe here," Sally told herself. "You won't have to gallop here."

For a while Sally searched the grounds for Misty, shouting about the dinners, walks and chocolate biscuits that were waiting for her if she would only come home. But there was no trace of Misty; no hairy face hung about with grasses and leaves peered through the undergrowth, no pad of paws announced her return. Ben had taken the dogs out that morning and Misty had done her usual disappearing trick. They had been in the walled garden and one second Misty had been with him, the next she had gone.

At last Sally gave up. She brought Willow in, meaning to ride down the avenue and search for Misty there. She groomed Willow, put on her tack, then went to get her hard hat from her room. She climbed the stairs, smoothing the carved Kestrels as she passed. She took her hard hat from its hook behind the door, then sat down on the window seat. Sea and sand stretched to blue sky and Sally was alone in the whole of Kestrels. Brightly coloured flags fluttered from the gymkhana tents. They would all be there now.

Instantly Sally looked away from the gymkhana. She searched the grounds of Kestrels and the fields beyond for any disturbance that might be Misty but there was no sign of her.

"Thalia thinks you're a coward," Sally told herself. "Afraid of everything. But it's not true. It's not true."

Sally picked up the crystal unicorn and set it in the centre of her hand, just as it had been when she had found it. She looked at it closely, giving it all her attention and suddenly she knew what she would do.

She would climb the tower. Her parents had forbidden any of them to go near the tower until the stair was renewed but Sally didn't care. She jumped down from the window seat and ran downstairs. Taking the ladder from the kitchen cupboard she clanged her way back and set the ladder squarely under the trap door. She clambered up, then hesitated. What would her mother say if she could see her now? But her mother would never know. No one would know. She had to climb the tower to prove to herself that she wasn't a coward.

Sally pushed the heavy trap door open. When the dust had settled she could see the stairs and the patch of blue sky above her head.

She breathed in hard, gritted her teeth and pulled herself up through the trap door to sit at the foot of the tower. The wood of the stairs was worse than Sally had remembered but the metal bannister seemed firm enough. Sally stood up cautiously and gripped the rusty metal. She shook it hard. Tatters of wood fell down but the bannister did not move. Holding onto the rail Sally stepped her way upwards, her feet between the spars.

As she climbed she heard wood and plaster falling down beneath her. A lump of rotted wood fell through the trap door and crashed to the floor below. For minutes she could not move – could only cling helplessly, her hands sticky with sweat, her mouth and throat bone dry.

"Get on, Sally Lorimer. Get on."

Trembling Sally forced herself to move one foot to the next rung, and then the next.

At last she reached the top and it was easy to step from the bannister to the broad stone platform that surrounded the tower.

Gripping the top of the tower Sally gazed out in total amazement. She could see round the curve of the globe – ocean and fields, farms, rough grazing, clumps of trees and church spires lay spread out beneath her. She could see beyond the gymkhana field to meadows and roads and white detached villas.

Looking away from the view Sally saw that there was a small metal chest stacked on the platform. Cautiously she made her way round to it. To her surprise it opened easily and was quite dry inside. As well as maps, playing cards and books there was a pair of binoculars in a leather case. Sally slipped the leather strap over her head and holding them to her eyes she focussed the blurred colours and the landscape leapt at her. She could see shells on the shore, blades of grass and the petals of flowers. She turned the binoculars onto the gymkhana and saw ponies and riders, red and white poles and a black pony jumping, sandwiches and lemonade on a trestle table with someone that that could only be Thalia's Narg ready to sell them.

She followed the line of the shore back towards Kestrels. A rough field reached down to the shore. A fence made of strands of wire surrounded it. Something was caught beneath the bottom strand of the wire. It struggled to free itself, its long grey and white hair fanned out as it threw itself desperately against the wire.

Sally focussed the glasses on it and there was Misty, so close that Sally felt she could almost touch her. Her eyes were wild with panic, her front feet clawed frantically at her neck as she fought to free herself. As Sally stared, hardly able to believe what she was seeing, Misty gave a sudden violent leap, then fell back from the wire and hung there motionless, so still she might have been dead.

Sally screamed Misty's name, dropped the binoculars back into their case, slammed the lid shut and was groping, stumbling her way down the bannister, jumping onto the ladder and leaping down to the floor in panic speed.

There was no one she could phone, no one to help her; the police too far away and too slow.

"Misty," Sally cried again. "Oh Misty."

Somehow Sally had to reach her and take her to a vet. Then she remembered that the vet would be at the gymkhana. There was only one way to reach him. She had to gallop Willow over the sands to Misty and find some way of taking her to the vet.

For a moment Sally was frozen with terror. Her legs would not move. She had to do the thing she dreaded most – to gallop over the sands. But it was for Misty. In her mind's eye she saw the limp hanging body. For Misty. And Sally drove the stupid fear out of her mind.

She spun into her room, grabbed her hard hat, thrust the unicorn deep into her pocket and tore downstairs. In the kitchen she snatched the kitchen scissors, dragged on her anorak and flew down to the stables.

"We've got to reach her now, at once," Sally cried as she pulled up Willow's girth and rushed her into the yard. As if she had been Thalia, Sally sprang into the saddle and pushed Willow into a canter as they plunged down the sandy track to the shore.

"On you go! On you go!" Sally cried. There was no space for fear, nothing in her head but the desperate need to reach Misty.

Willow's hooves pounded into the sands, her long mane and tail bannered about her as Sally crouched low and tight over her neck, urging her on.

They reached the field where Misty was trapped and Sally pulled Willow to a plunging halt. She threw herself from the saddle and knowing she should never do it, looped Willow's reins over one of the fence posts, then flung herself across the field to where Misty hung unconscious from the wire fence. Sally crouched down beside her and saw that she had put her head through a noose trap that hung from the bottom strand of wire. Sally's fingers searched desperately through Misty's thick ruff of hair until she found the nylon noose. She gnawed through it with the scissors and Misty's limp body fell to the ground.

Sally stared down helplessly. Misty's eyes were closed, her tongue lolling from the side of her mouth, her breath harsh and uneven. She was still alive.

"The vet," Sally thought. "Got to get her to the vet. NOW."

And hardly knowing what she was going to do, Sally pulled off her anorak, spread it out and laid Misty on top of it. She zipped it up and knotted the sleeves together. Carrying the warm, limp body in her arms she staggered back to Willow.

"It's only Misty," she told the grey pony. "Only Misty. You know her. It's all right," and Willow breathed over the strange bundle, then whinnied gently, letting Sally know that she understood.

Somehow Sally hoisted Misty over her pony's withers, somehow held her there as she scrambled back into the saddle. Clutching onto Misty she managed to turn Willow back to the beach.

"Gallop," Sally told her. "Go on, gallop. You've got to get us to the gymkhana, got to get us to the vet," and she urged Willow on.

Sally had thought she could have held onto Misty with one hand and held her reins with the other but it took both hands to stop the lolling, unconscious Beardie from falling off. Sally had to leave her reins loose, was only able to guide Willow with her legs.

Straight and true Willow galloped across the sands, never hesitating or trying to turn back. She raced up the short lane to the gymkhana field and plunged through the entrance.

"I've got to see the vet," Sally screamed at the amazed spectators. "It's urgent, really urgent," and in seconds Mr Cheever stood beside her. He lifted Misty up out of the anorak and carried her to his Land Rover. He laid her down on the grass and examined her.

"It was a noose," Sally explained as she slackened Willow's girth, eased her saddle and clapped her sweated neck, praising her and thanking her for her bold galloping. "Some sort of trap."

"I'd swing them up on their own bloomin' traps," swore the vet.

"Is she all right? Is she going to be all right?" Sally demanded.

"Her thick coat's saved her. Been a smooth coated dog you'd have lost her," answered the vet.

He took a syringe out of his case and filling it, injected Misty.

"That will give her heart a bit of a boost. She'll come round in a few moments."

"It is Sally," yelled Thalia as she trotted Tarquin towards them, Em running at her side.

"What's happened?" asked Em. "What's wrong with Misty?"

Sally blurted out her story.

"You mean you galloped over the sands?" exclaimed Thalia, ignoring everything else. "You really galloped?"

Em went to find their parents and by the time she returned with them Misty had opened her eyes, sat up, scratched herself and peed.

"She'll be all right," said the vet. "Keep her quiet for a bit and keep an eye on her from now on. You were lucky this time. Next time you could be too late. I'll call in this evening and check up on her."

Sally repeated her story and her mother said they would have a talk about climbing the tower stair later.

"But Sally galloped," insisted Thalia. "She's not afraid any longer."

Sally listened to their praises, not really hearing them. What mattered was that she had escaped from the blackness of being afraid; that Misty was safe and that Willow, her own pony, was the best possibly pony in the whole world.

They were making their way back to the Lorimers' car, Misty walking beside Meg as if nothing had happened to her, Jamie with a lollipop in each hand, when Thalia shouted, "Musical poles! They've not started yet and I entered Sally."

In minutes Sally found herself trotting round the ring with twelve other children, ready to ride into the centre and put her hard hat on a pole when the tape stopped playing. Willow listened to the music; spun round and cantered to a pole the second it stopped. She kept Sally in until fourth place. Sally's rosette, her first rosette, was yellow with gold lettering. Thalia's was blue for second place.

When the gymkhana was over Sally and Thalia rode home together. Mrs Lorimer had invited Thalia and Narg for a picnic supper in the summerhouse.

"We'll need to see about our entries for the Tarent Show," said Thalia. "I'll ask my Narg to find out about them."

"Oh yes," agreed Sally, then stopped, giggling at herself for she hadn't even thought of being afraid.

"Do you think Willow can jump?" Thalia asked. "She looks to me as if she could."

"Well I can't" said Sally.

"Of course you can," said Thalia. "Jumping's easy as long as your pony enjoys it. I'll show you."

As they walked their ponies slowly back to Kestrels, Sally's imagination dazzled with thoughts of jumping Willow, of Tarent Show and of her crystal unicorn, secure in her pocket, that seemed to have cast its rainbow magic over her whole life.

"Thank you," she said aloud. "Thank you," and she rode through sky and sea-light home to Kestrels and into a future filled with ponies.